HORSES

understanding
ANIMALS

By
Dorothy
Hinshaw
Patent

photos
by
William
Muñoz

Carolrhoda Books, Inc.
Minneapolis

To horse lovers everywhere
                    −DHP

To Suzanne
          −WM

The author and photographer wish to thank the following people for their help with this book: Donna Hyora, Pryor Mountain Wild Horse Refuge, Suzanne Mulberger, Sean Muñoz, Sandy Muñoz, David and Beverly Tarmina, Julie and Harold Bangs, Pat Miller, Jill Fairchild, Jane Spahr, Rita Cunningham, Roland Moore, Minnesota Zoo, Ingrid Stevenson, and Dale Mahlum.

Additional photographs courtesy of: p. 8 (left) French Government Tourist Office; pp. 18, 21, 36, Dorothy Hinshaw Patent

Words that appear in **bold** type are listed in the glossary on page 47.

Ruth Berman, Series Editor
Zachary Marell, Series Designer

Library of Congress Cataloging-in-Publication Data

Patent, Dorothy Hinshaw.
    Horses / by Dorothy Hinshaw Patent ; photographs by William Muñoz.
        p.   cm. − (Understanding Animals)
    Includes index.
    Summary: Discusses the physical characteristics and behavior of horses and describes how domestic horses evolved from their wild relatives.
        ISBN 0-87614-766-X
    1. Horses—Behavior—Juvenile literature. 2. Wild horses—Behavior—Juvenile literature. 3. Horses—Juvenile literature. 4. Wild Horses—Juvenile literature. [1. Horses—Habits and behavior.] I. Muñoz, William, ill. II. Title. III. Series.
SF281.P38 1994
636.1—dc20   93-12329
                                                         CIP
                                                          AC

Manufactured in the United States of America

1 2 3 4 5 6 − P/MP − 99 98 97 96 95 94

Contents

Chapter 1

.
.
.

Horses and Wild Horses

.
.
.

Over time, people have bred big, powerful horses like the Percherons (opposite), and tiny ones like the miniature horse above.

*H*orses, horses, horses—people love these beautiful, powerful creatures. We enjoy them when they are tame, giving us the pleasure of riding on their backs into parks and woodlands. We also value the image of them wild, roaming across the landscape at will, free from our control.

Horses come in many shapes and sizes. There are delicate miniature horses, less than 34 inches tall at the shoulder. Ponies are bigger—up to 58 inches tall. Saddle horses like the agile quarter horse and the swift Thoroughbred are big enough to carry the weight of a saddle and an adult person. Big, heavy draft horses like Clydesdales and Percherons can weigh over a ton and stand 72 inches at the shoulder. These animals are strong enough to pull loaded wagons and heavy farm equipment with ease.

Above: *This horse was painted on the wall of Lascaux Cave, in France, around 15,000 B.C.*

ORIGIN OF THE HORSE

Where do all these kinds of horses come from? This is a difficult question. Experts cannot agree on whether horses have a variety of wild ancestors or just one. Since all familiar breeds of horses can interbreed and produce healthy offspring who can also breed, they are considered to belong to the same species, *Equus caballus.* Today, only one species of truly wild horse survives, the Przewalski's (puhr-zheh-VAHL-skihz) horse, usually called *Equus przewalski* by scientists.

In recent times, the Przewalski's horse was found only on the dry Eurasian grasslands called the steppe. But this hardy animal may once have roamed over Europe and other parts of Asia as well. Cave paintings made by prehistoric people in France and Spain include horses along with other wild animals of the time. Some of the horses resemble the Przewalski's horse, with short legs, short bodies, heavy heads, and thick necks with upright manes. They also have yellowish tan bodies and dark manes, tails, and lower legs like Przewalski's horses. Chances are these prehistoric horses were gradually driven from Europe by hunters, who valued their meat.

Right: *The Przewalski's horse is the only true wild horse that exists today.*

The Norwegian fjord horse looks very much like the Przewalski's horse and is about the same size.

Prehistoric people weren't the only ones to hunt horses. Even in the 18th century, hunting parties of Mongolian emperors would kill as many as 300 Przewalski's horses in one day. Hunting continued until at least 1949, driving the species to extinction in the wild. The last verified wild sighting was in 1968. Fortunately, Przewalski's horses do well in captivity, and herds thrive at several zoos around the world. Both Russia and the People's Republic of China are working on reintroducing the animals into the wild.

Draft horses and some pony breeds today are heavily built and have strong, thick necks like the Przewalski's horse and the horses that were most commonly drawn by prehistoric artists. But there are also lightly built breeds with long, slender legs and necks. Where did they come from? Cave paintings in France show some horses that appear smaller and more refined than the Przewalski's type. But the more delicate breeds of horses, such as Arabians, most likely originated in Asia.

We do know of at least one other wild horse, called the tarpan, that lived in Europe until recent times. The tarpan was mouse gray and had a dark stripe running down its back. It had an upright black mane, black tail, and dark face. During the winter, its coat turned shaggy and lighter in color. The tarpan inhabited the forests and fertile plains of central Europe. Tarpans are the ancestors of native Polish ponies, called *koniks*. Like the Przewalski's horse, tarpans were hunted for their tasty meat. During the 1700s, tarpans were also hunted because the **stallions,** or males, stole domestic **mares,** or females. The last tarpans disappeared in the mid-1800s.

After World War I, a Polish scientist decided to recreate the tarpan. He studied writings about tarpans and selected koniks that looked and behaved as much like them as possible. But World War II brought destruction, and the project was begun all over again in the 1950s. Today, tarpanlike horses roam the last remnants of European forests in Poland. Unlike the original tarpans, the "reconstructed" tarpans have a mane that falls over the neck.

The Przewalski's horse is a possible ancestor of modern-day horses.

Horses, such as this Bashkir Curly, are still used to pull buggies, just as they once pulled the war chariots of invaders in Asia and Europe.

The tarpan and the Przewalski's horse are both possible ancestors of modern-day horses. But there may have been others as well—species that were killed off in the wild before people could write about them.

TAMING THE HORSE

No one knows just where and when horses were first **tamed.** Horse bones are found associated with humans in prehistoric sites. But since early peoples hunted wild horses for their meat, it is difficult to know if these bones are of tamed animals. Chances are, horses were tamed in a number of different locations in Europe and Asia between 4500 and 2500 B.C. By 1000 B.C., horses had become an important part of life for people in North Africa, Europe, and Asia.

Horses were probably used for pulling wagons and chariots before they were ridden. The use of horses brought about a revolution in warfare. Soldiers in chariots could swoop down swiftly on their horseless enemies, who were almost helpless in comparison.

Social interactions are important to Przewalski's horses (right) and domesticated horses alike.

Below: *Handling horses from the time they are young foals makes them as comfortable with people as possible.*

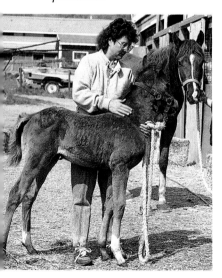

The horse also sped up human opportunities for trade. Like cattle, horses could transport heavy loads, but they could move much more rapidly. The horse's strength, stamina, and speed opened up new trade routes and expanded the communication among different peoples on earth.

What made taming the horse possible? If a young wild animal is raised by humans, it loses its fear of people and becomes tame. Most wild animals that are dependent on their mothers in their early days can be at least partially tamed. Animals that live naturally in social groups are easier to tame than solitary ones. Such creatures are used to relating to others of their own kind. They can transfer some of their social behavior to their relationships with humans. And when people learn what signals the animals use to communicate with one another, we can tune in and decode the "animal talk." But relatively few animal species have been truly **domesticated,** a process that takes generations to achieve.

Domestication involves more than taming. In a domesticated animal, the inherited behavioral tendencies of the species have actually changed so that individuals of the species are generally easy to tame. As adults, domesticated animals accept humans and will stay around human habitations. The inborn caution of wild animals is largely gone. Individuals of some domesticated species, such as dogs, cats, and horses, can develop rich emotional relationships with their human companions.

Some domesticated animals, such as the majority of dogs, have changed so much over generations that they can no longer survive without human care and protection. Such animals must always look to us to meet their needs. But horses are different. As one of the most recently domesticated animals, horses have in many ways changed little from their wild ancestors. Almost any breed, from heavy draft horses to small ponies, could survive in the wild if need be. Perhaps only the recently developed miniature horse would be an exception.

Foals are curious.

Opposite and Above: *Feral horses*

Chapter 2

Horses in the Wild

Whenit comes to horses, the word *wild* is usually misused. A truly wild species is one that has always lived wild, with only wild ancestors. When a domesticated species escapes and manages to survive without human care, it is properly called **feral,** not wild. There are feral cats, pigs, goats, and horses, to name the principal animals that have escaped from domestication in some areas.

When horses are freed from human control, they revert to the ancient habits of their wild origins. They still know the old ways of survival and social life, even though their ancestors have been domesticated for thousands of years.

Wild horses once roamed freely throughout the western United States. Now they are limited to small areas in only a few states.

HORSES COME TO AMERICA

The ancestors of horses lived in North and South America at one time, but they died out over 8,000 years ago, before horses were domesticated anywhere in the world. But when Spanish explorers in the 15th century landed in South America and Mexico, horses began their return to the Americas. Later, in the 1600s, settlers at Spanish missions in the Rio Grande Valley brought livestock with them, including horses. These settlements extended up into what is now New Mexico. It didn't take long before some of the horses escaped from their owners and became feral. The rich prairies and plains of the American West were a perfect place for a grazing animal like the horse, and soon feral horses were abundant.

Meanwhile, the Spanish settlers forced local Indians into slavery and taught them how to take care of the horses. The Spaniards knew how useful horses could be in fighting, however, so they didn't allow the Indians to ride. They didn't want to give the power of the horse to their slaves. But the Indians observed how horses could be controlled and ridden, and it wasn't long before they had developed their own methods of working with these useful animals. This knowledge was passed on to free Indians.

The animals weren't hard for the free Indians to come by. Horses could be stolen quite easily, or goods could be traded for them. Feral horses could be captured, tamed, and brought under human control. Use of the horse completely transformed the lives of the Plains Indians, giving them a strong pack animal and a swift teammate for hunting and warfare.

The Appaloosa, a breed with a variety of spotted patterns, was developed by the Nez Perce Indians.

WILD HORSES TODAY

Today, there are no truly wild horses living in North or South America. But feral horses do exist. While *feral* is the correct term for domesticated horses gone wild, the word *wild* is so commonly accepted that it will be used here. Wild horses roam in 10 western states. Arizona, Colorado, Idaho, Montana, and New Mexico have a few. California, Oregon, and Utah have more, and Wyoming has quite a large number. Nevada, however, is home to more than half the wild horses in the United States. One reason is that most of the land in Nevada is publicly owned. It is open and unfenced, so the horses can roam freely.

The United States isn't the only area where domesticated horses have returned to the wild. Wild horses also live in parts of western Canada and in Australia. In France, at the mouth of the Rhone River, lives a special breed of horse called the Camargue. The **foals,** or babies, are born black or brown but turn to white between three and eight years of age. The animals live wild, but local people take some of the stallions and use them for riding.

Wild horses in Nevada

Even though these wild horses live in one area, they group together in their own bands.

In Britain, some kinds of ponies are left to their own devices for most of the year, living much like wild horses. The Exmoor ponies, for example, are rounded up once a year. The animals are inspected, and ponies with the most authentic Exmoor traits are released again. The others are sold for use as riding and harness horses.

HORSE FAMILIES

Horses are social animals. Given a choice, a horse prefers living with others of its kind to living alone. In the wild, horses associate with one another in small family groups called **bands.** A typical band of wild horses consists of a mature stallion, one or more adult mares, and the offspring of those mares that are up to three years old. Each horse in the band has its rank in relation to the other animals. The stallion is **dominant** over all the others. That means all the horses in the band do what the stallion "tells" them to do. Another way of expressing this relationship is to say that the other horses in the band are **subordinate** to the stallion and may show **submissive** behavior toward him.

Young horses leave the band starting when they are about two years old. When a young female horse is ready to breed, the dominant stallion, generally her father, chases her away. Young stallions form small bachelor bands. Young stallions are always on the lookout for young mares and may fight over them. Once one stallion has been able to claim a mare, a new band has begun. A young mare may also become part of an established band.

STALLIONS

The stallion protects his band from danger, often standing a little apart from the others, watching out while they graze. If danger threatens, the stallion snorts in warning and may circle the band to get the horses moving away from the danger. Sometimes he leads them as they gallop off. Other times, a top-ranking mare leads while the stallion takes up the rear, ready to fight if need be to protect his band.

A stallion is always on the alert for other stallions, since they may steal his mares if he isn't careful. But because most stallions do carefully protect their bands from rivals, mares aren't

Below: *A slight disagreement in a bachelor band*

Right: *The stallion stands apart from his band and watches out for danger.*

stolen very often. If stallions spot one another, they stare at and approach each other, prancing and tossing their heads. When the stallions meet, they sniff at one another. The sniffing may be intense, beginning at the head and working along the body, snuffling noisily all the way. They may give loud squeals and paw at the ground.

In any area, the stallions usually know one another well. Most encounters between male horses are limited to neck arching and prancing. If a bachelor stallion encounters a band, chances are he knows that the leader is stronger than he is and will turn away to avoid a fight. But if he senses that his rival may have become weaker with age, or that his own strength may have increased enough to win a fight, he won't back down.

The Przewalski's stallion is leading his band away from possible danger. Notice that the foals stay close to him for protection.

Right: *Two stallions begin a minor fight.*

Above: *Many of the movements in dressage, during which a trained horse performs on command, are derived from the horse's natural behavior. Here, in an extended trot, the horse moves forward with its neck arched as if displaying before a rival or a mare.*

When stallions fight, they rear up on their hind legs, strike out with their hooves, and bite at each other's necks. They also circle around, trying to bite one another's rear legs. Sometimes they get down on their knees and try to bite each other's forelegs. They may break off contact and prance together, necks arched and hooves lifted high. Eventually, one or the other gives up, turns away, and is chased off.

When a stallion encounters a mare that is ready to breed, he shows off in some of the same ways. He approaches her from the front, neck gracefully arched and nostrils flaring. The two horses sniff at each other. The stallion may prance along beside the mare, chin tucked in, knees raising up as he trots.

GROWING UP

Young horses in the wild are born in the springtime. A few weeks after giving birth, the mother horse is ready to breed again and will have another foal in about 11 months. In that way, she has a new baby once a year at about the same time.

Mares usually separate themselves from the band when they give birth, finding a quiet, secluded place. Most births take place under the protective cover of darkness.

The mare lies on her side to give birth. The foal is born front feet first, with its head tucked between them. Birth takes only a few minutes. Once the foal is born, the mare rolls onto her stomach and reaches back to nuzzle the foal, nickering to it softly. Then she stands up and licks her new baby.

The foal tries to stand up almost immediately after birth, struggling to get its long legs to cooperate. As soon as it is on its feet, the young horse nuzzles its mother's body, looking for the teats from which it can suck warm, sweet milk.

Above: *A newborn foal with its mother.*

Left: *A wild mare and her foal.*

Below: *The mare is protective of her foal.*

Horses are born strong. Within an hour and a half, the new foal is able to stand, walk, and nurse. By the time it is three hours old, it can trot and gallop and is ready to play with other youngsters. Within a few hours of birth, the mother leads her new baby back to the band, where it becomes acquainted with the other animals.

The mare is very protective of her foal. If she feels that another member of the band, such as a curious yearling, might harm her baby, she will chase it away. The lead stallion is tolerant of the foals and protects them along with the rest of the band.

SOCIAL LIFE

Social relationships in the band are important to horses. Foals may spend hours romping and playing together. Brothers can be close friends with one another, as can sisters. Mares have special relationships with their own offspring, even after they have grown up. The result is a society based on dominance, family relationships, and friendship.

Right: *These older foals are ready to romp and play.*

Opposite: *Grooming*

Foals and adults alike show their caring concern for one another through grooming. Grooming behavior probably helps get rid of bothersome insects. But it also appears to feel good for its own sake. When a horse wants to be groomed, it approaches another horse in its band from the front. The two sniff noses and necks, then begin nibbling at each other's necks. They work their way down their backs all the way to the tail bases. Grooming usually lasts just a few minutes. When finished, the animals may trade sides and groom once more, or they may just stand companionably close together, grazing or dozing.

Right: *Two horses cooper-*
ate in swishing away flies.

Below: *Wild horses spend*
most of their time grazing.

Horses also help one another in the war against insects by standing head to tail, each animal energetically swishing its tail to discourage the flies that are trying to bite its companion.

FOOD AND DRINK

Horses are able to live in places with little food and water. The Red Desert of Wyoming and the vast sagebrush deserts of Nevada are home to thousands of wild horses. But the animals must spend most of their time grazing, since they need to eat about 25 pounds of grass each day.

Water is very important to wild horses. In some areas, there are so few water holes that the horses can drink only every two or three days. When the band reaches a water hole, the stallion waits to one side, guarding while the rest of the band drinks. If several bands arrive around the same time, they take turns drinking. A band with a more dominant stallion will get to drink before one with a subordinate leader.

Water holes like this one are vital to the survival of wild horses.

BEING A HORSE

This mare is alert, watching out for trouble while her foal nurses.

Some people scorn horses, saying that they are flighty and panic easily. Such folk may compare horses to animals such as dogs and cats, which are likely to face the world with curiosity rather than caution. But the attitudes of animals are shaped

by their roles in the wild. Dogs and cats are predators by nature. They need to seek out their prey and be willing to
attack, often at great risk to their own lives. Prey animals like
horses, on the other hand, need to be wary to survive. They
must be constantly watchful and suspicious, keeping a lookout
for danger. Much of the behavior of horses can be explained
through an understanding of their role in nature as prey animals. For example, people often are frustrated by a horse that
shies easily at a sudden movement. Such an action may cause
trouble for a rider, but in nature it could save a horse's life.

These young horses are skittish, ready to run off because of a sudden sound or movement.

Above: *People and horses can communicate through touch.*

Opposite: *A horse has a special relationship with every other horse in its band.*

Chapter 3

How Horses Communicate

S ocial animals need ways to communicate with one an-other. We humans mostly use our voices, speaking hundreds of different languages around the world. Sight is also important in our communication—a frown, a shrug of the shoulders, or the energetic nodding of the head can express as much as dozens of words. Touch can say a great deal—a hug at the right time lets us know that someone is there to help us when we need it most.

Horses as well as humans use sight, sound, and touch to get messages across. Like many other animals, they also use smell, a sense that we tend to ignore. If you know what to listen and look for when you are around horses, you can understand a great deal about what they are feeling. You can also get an idea as to what they might do next.

Horses always notice new things in their environment.

HORSES AND SOUNDS

Horses can hear higher pitched sounds than we can. They use sound to get across important messages to one another. Their most familiar sound is the whinny, or neigh.

Whinnies can be heard more than a half mile away, and horses use them for long-distance communication. Each individual has its own distinctive neigh, which its friends and family can recognize. If a horse is separated from its companions, it may whinny to find out where they are. The answering neigh gives their location. Mares are especially responsive to the whinnies of their own foals.

The nicker is a gentle horse greeting that is broken up into soft syllables. Horses greet one another and their human friends with nickers at close range. Mares keep in touch with their foals with nickers, gently telling them to stay close by. Stallions courting mares use a special long, low-pitched nicker to express their interest.

When one horse feels threatened by another, it may squeal a warning. You might hear a squeal when horses are jostling one another at a feed trough or if a mare wants to avoid an approaching stallion's advances. If two stallions are in the early stages of a fight, they may squeal at each other.

When a wild horse detects potential danger, it snorts a warning to the members of the band. A snort from a band member will bring all heads up from grazing, and the animals will look in the same direction, ready to flee if necessary.

WATCHING HORSES

The sensitive ears of a horse can be a good indicator of its mood. When a horse is dozing, its ears are flopped over to the sides with their openings downward. If a horse that isn't sleeping is holding its ears this way, it may be very tired or even unwell. In social encounters, a horse will droop its ears as a sign of giving in to another horse that is trying to dominate it.

Always on the alert, even while grazing, horses turn their ears toward a source of noise.

Below: *The position of the ears is a dead giveaway that this horse is alert to the goings-on in its environment.*

An alert horse, on the other hand, has ears standing straight up and pricked forward. The ears may swivel independently of each other, this way and that, trying to locate the direction of a sound. Horses can even turn their ears around so that they face backward to pick up noises from behind. The alert ears of horses are one of their secrets of success in the wild. Prey animals need to be constantly aware of their surroundings so they can run off at a moment's notice when danger threatens.

When a horse is feeling aggressive, it shows its intentions by laying its ears flat against its head. If you are trying to get acquainted with a horse and it lays its ears back, don't reach out toward its head—it might bite.

Right: *The horse on the left has its ears laid back in warning that it might bite.*

Left: *A startled Shetland foal*

While horses don't have faces that are as expressive as people's, you can still tell a great deal about how a horse is feeling from its mouth and eyes. Frightened or aggressive horses may raise their heads up and roll their eyes so that the white part shows. Pulled-back lips that reveal teeth produce a bite threat. But if a young horse pulls back its lips and clacks its teeth together, it is a submissive gesture.

A stallion gets a strange look on his face when he smells the urine of a mare to see if she is ready to mate. He stretches his head forward and curls his top lip upward, showing the upper gums as well as the teeth. This gesture, known by the German word *flehmen,* seems to open up the channels to special organs of smell located on the roof of the mouth. Once in a while, a foal or mare will exhibit flehmen in response to a strange odor.

Above: *Even though he's young, a male foal exhibits flehmen.*

Right: *The Przewalski's mare with a carrot in her mouth is tossing her head, annoyed at the interest the other horses show in her prize.*

Above: *The Przewalski's mare on the left has her head down and her front foot raised in a kicking threat.*

Horses also show their moods in the way they carry their heads. The courting stallion arches his neck gracefully, chin tucked in, which shows off his strength and beauty. A tired horse stands with drooping head and neck, while a horse that objects to what is going on may toss its head up and down or shake it from side to side. A horse being saddled up often tosses and shakes its head as the saddle is thrown on, or as the cinch is tightened.

If a horse isn't happy to be saddled up, it may also show its objections by stamping one of its front feet. Making a thumping sound by knocking the ground with one of the hind feet is a mild warning. If a horse lifts one leg and holds it there, it may be letting you know that it might kick or strike out if you don't move away.

A horse's tail can also reveal quite a bit about the animal's mood. Most of the time, the tail hangs down in a relaxed way or is used to swish away bothersome insects. But if a horse is tense or angry, it may elevate the base of the tail so that it sticks straight out behind, making the tail hang away from the body. If the horse then begins to flick its tail back and forth, watch out! It may be ready to kick. A horse turning its body so that its rump is toward you can be another warning of a potential kick.

The way a horse carries its tail is a sign of its mood. The tail of the horse above tells us that the horse is relaxed, whereas the tail of the horse at left is a sign that the horse is excited.

Nowadays, people ride horses for pleasure (above), or use horses to pull wagons on pleasure trips through the countryside (opposite).

Chapter 4

Horses in Today's World

I n the western world, horses are better off today than they were before machines replaced them as work animals. When horses were the main source of energy for pulling wagons and plowing fields, they were looked upon as necessary possessions rather than as feeling animals. Certainly, there have always been horse lovers, people who enjoy working with horses and taking good care of them. But there were also those who didn't care properly for their equine associates and who didn't treat them with compassion.

Today, horses are a luxury in western countries. Most of them are used for pleasure rather than work and are owned by people who love and respect them. People who use work horses for tasks such as farming do so by choice, not necessity.

Some horses, however, have jobs that worry people concerned about animal welfare. Carriage horses giving rides to tourists in some cities are one cause for concern: Do they work too hard? Do they have ready access to fresh water when they need it? Racehorses and rodeo horses, especially the bucking horses, are some other causes for concern: Are these animals forced to suffer pain in their work?

Above: *Some people are concerned about the treatment of horses in rodeos.*

Right: *Some farmers prefer to use horses like these Belgians rather than use machinery.*

Left: *Grazing in the pasture with other horses is satisfying.*

UNDERSTANDING HORSES' NEEDS

Even horses owned by people who care can have lonely, frustrating lives if their needs are not met. Horses are naturally social, so a horse living most of the time in a stall or by itself in the pasture is a lonely animal. This need for companionship is so strong that some racehorses are given another animal to keep them company. Goats are often chosen, and a racehorse can become very attached to its unusual friend.

Horses are also adapted to spending most of their time cropping grass. In nature, it takes many hours of grazing for a horse to get enough to eat. But a horse kept in a barn and fed hay and grain can have its food needs met in a very short feeding period. Once its food is gone, there is almost no way for such a horse to entertain itself, and extreme boredom can settle in.

Above: *Buddies*

Above: *A horse by itself in a stall can get lonely.*

The combined frustration of being alone, feeding for only a short while, and being confined can lead to strange behavior. A common problem with stabled horses is **cribbing.** The animal bites the bars of its stall and inhales big gulps of air, leading to indigestion and irregular tooth wear. A bored confined horse may also weave back and forth like a caged zoo animal or become bad tempered. Exercising the horse every day helps relieve boredom. Placing hay in a net or rack so that the animal can pull out only a few strands at a time helps prolong feeding. A horse will also play with plastic jugs hanging in its stall and enjoys looking out its stall door.

Right: *Racehorses often exercise alone, which is better than no exercise at all.*

The pasture is a more normal place for a horse to live. There, it can graze, smell the air, and run. But even in a pasture, a lone horse is not living naturally. Whenever possible, a horse should have at least one other horse to keep it company. The two may act like rivals when their owner appears, flattening their ears and threatening one another, but they are still friends and companions the rest of the time.

Domestic horses form groups similar to wild bands if left to themselves in a pasture.

WILD HORSES IN AMERICA

When there is enough food to eat and enough water to drink, wild horses can reproduce at a very rapid pace. They can quickly outgrow the available resources and be in danger of starvation. In places where wild horses share the land with cattle, competing for resources, ranchers usually want the

Above: *Wild horses can multiply quickly when they have plenty of food and water.*

Opposite top: *This wild horse is being lassoed as part of the adoption process.*

Opposite bottom: *Capturing a wild horse in a roundup*

number of horses kept as low as possible. Groups of people who act to defend wild horses, however, want more horses on the land. The government is caught between these groups.

The Bureau of Land Management (BLM) is the government agency that manages most of the lands where wild horses live in the United States. Altogether, the BLM is responsible for more than 50,000 wild horses. In order to control the number of horses, roundups are planned in areas the BLM has decided are overpopulated with horses. After the horses are captured, some are released and others are held for adoption. When wild horses are captured young, they usually adapt quickly to domesticated life.

Anyone over the age of 18 can adopt up to four horses each year if he or she has an adequate place to keep and care for them. Each horse costs $125. For a year, the horse cannot be used as a bucking horse, sold for slaughter to be turned into pet food, or sold to someone else. After the person has taken good care of the horse for a year, the government gives him or her title to it. Then the horse can be used however the person chooses.

The BLM has adoption centers all across the country. From 1972, when the Adopt-A-Horse program began, through 1991, more than 90,000 wild horses have found homes with people.

Although horses, wild or tame, can take care of themselves very well, they also have an inborn ability to become friends and cooperate with a completely different species—our own. This special trait has led many people into close and rewarding relationships with this beautiful and useful social animal. For us, the horse's friendship and willingness to work are gifts from nature that we need to respect and appreciate.

Horses and ponies can be gentle friends for people as well as one another.

Glossary

band: a small family group of horses

cribbing: the bad habit of biting on the bars of stalls and gulping in air displayed by bored horses. Cribbing can lead to indigestion and irregular tooth wear. Also called crib biting.

domesticated: to have shaped a species of animal over time to live with and assist humans

dominant: higher in rank in the social order. A dominant animal has first access to resources such as a mate or food. Animals below it in rank are said to be subordinate, and they exhibit submissive behavior toward the dominant animal.

feral: living wild after having been domesticated

foals: baby horses

mares: female horses

stallions: male horses

submissive: behavior reflecting a lower rank

subordinate: occupying a lower rank or position

tame: to accustom an individual animal to the presence of humans

METRIC CONVERSION CHART		
WHEN YOU KNOW:	MULTIPLY BY:	TO FIND:
inches	2.54	centimeters
miles	1.609	kilometers
pounds	.454	kilograms
tons	.907	metric tons

Index

Pages listed in **bold** type refer to photographs.